I Love Ugali and Sukuma Wiki

Written and Illustrated by
Kwame Nyong'o

Dedicated to my grandmother, Mama Dorcas,
who makes the best *ugali* and *sukuma wiki*
in the world!

I Love Ugali and Sukuma Wiki

Habari! My name is Akiki and I live in a small village in Kenya. I want to tell you about my favourite dish. It's called *ugali* and *sukuma wiki*.

You're probably wondering, What is *ugali*?
What is *sukuma wiki*? *Ugali* is a traditional food common in Kenya and other parts of Africa. It's made of maize flour which is boiled into a firm cake.

To eat it, you squash it up and make it into little cups. You then dip these cups into the *sukuma wiki* and then pop it all into your mouth. Mmmh!

I like *ugali* best with ... *sukuma wiki! Sukuma wiki* is a green leaved vegetable which looks a bit like spinach. It's usually cooked into a stew with onions and tomatoes.

My Grandma makes the best *sukuma wiki*! She chops up and fries the tomatoes and onions in her pot over a hot charcoal *jiko*. The *jiko* gives the food that mmm-aah-mazing home cooked taste!

She then cuts up the *sukuma wiki* into tiny, tiny pieces. After adding some water and a dash of salt, she boils it for about twenty minutes…then…it's ready!

Some very delicious and wonderful *sukuma wiki*!
Ready to eat with *ugali*!

I love my Grandma and her cooking. I love making the *ugali* into those small cups, dipping them into the *sukuma wiki* then dunking it all together into my mouth. I heard they call it *sukuma wiki* because that means 'push the week' in Swahili. And it really does get so many people through the week because it is easy to grow, cheap to buy and fun to eat!

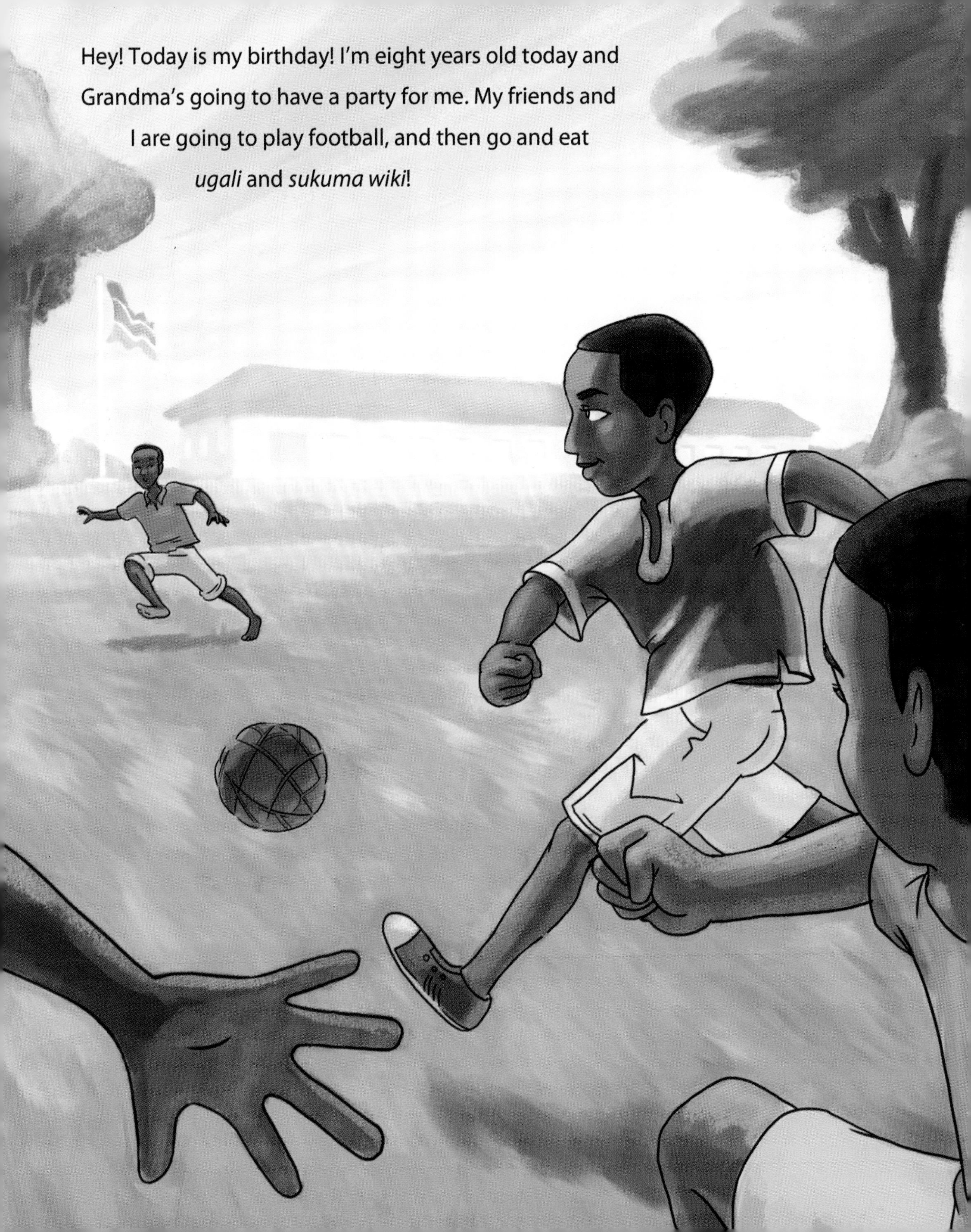

Hey! Today is my birthday! I'm eight years old today and Grandma's going to have a party for me. My friends and I are going to play football, and then go and eat *ugali* and *sukuma wiki*!

After the party, Grandma pulled me aside. "Akiki, I know you love your *ugali* and *sukuma wiki* and I'm glad you eat it so much. It has helped you grow big and strong, giving you all the energy you need to kick those footballs. But now that you're eight years old, you'll have to start using some of your free time during the school holidays to help me grow vegetables in our *shamba*."

"What!" I thought to myself in disappointment. I liked playing football all day with my friends during the holidays! Working in the *shamba* seemed boring!

"I don't want to be in the *shamba*, I want to play with the other kids in the village during school breaks," I mumbled.

But Grandma told me. "Now Akiki, ask yourself, where will we get *ugali* and *sukuma wiki* from if we don't work in our shamba and grow the maize, kale, tomatoes and the onions?"

"Oh, ok, I'll try," I reluctantly accepted.

I was upset but I helped out in the *shamba* during the next school holidays. I dug the *shamba* with a *jembe* in the morning...

... and then was free to play with my friends in the afternoon!

Within a short time, I found that working in the *shamba* not so boring after all. It became exciting to think that what I was doing would turn into *sukuma wiki* and other vegetables before long.

It was soon planting season. I enjoyed planting the seeds, and seeing them sprout after the rains passed over. I learned that it's best to buy and use certified seed when planting. That gives the best chance of germinating and growing well.

In three months, it will be time to harvest!

I also learned that *sukuma wiki* needs to be protected from insects and pests by spraying pyrethrum on the leaves. Pyrethrum is a natural insecticide and prevents the insects from eating the leaves of the *sukuma wiki* as it grows.

Three months later, and the school holidays are back. Wow! It's finally time to harvest the *sukuma wiki*!

We picked all the maize and dried it under the sun. We then shelled them, removing all the kernels from the husks.

Later, we put all the maize into a *gunia* and took it over to the local *posho* mill. The big machine at the mill then ground the maize up into flour... *ugali* flour!

We then picked the *sukuma wiki*, the tomatoes, the onions. After we had all our ingredients together, Grandma let me help her cook! I stirred the *ugali* with Grandma's *mwiko*. It took a lot of muscle to do so because the *ugali* gets firmer and firmer the more you stir it.

Grandma made the *sukuma wiki* with an extra treat: cubes of meat inside! Mmmh! I was so hungry now!

Grandpa came back from safari. He was escorted by my aunties Auma and Patience as well as my favourite cousin, Musa!

We sat down together at the supper table. Grandpa prayed then we began to eat. I tell you the food was amazing...so tasty! I made fist after fist of *ugali* bowls and dipped them in my *sukuma wiki*. The flavour was so incredible! It melted on my tongue, slid down my throat and entered my *tumbo*. It was the best *ugali* and *sukuma wiki* I have ever had.

I hope you too will get a chance to eat *ugali* and *sukuma wiki* one day. It's an experience you'll never, ever forget...

Map of Kenya

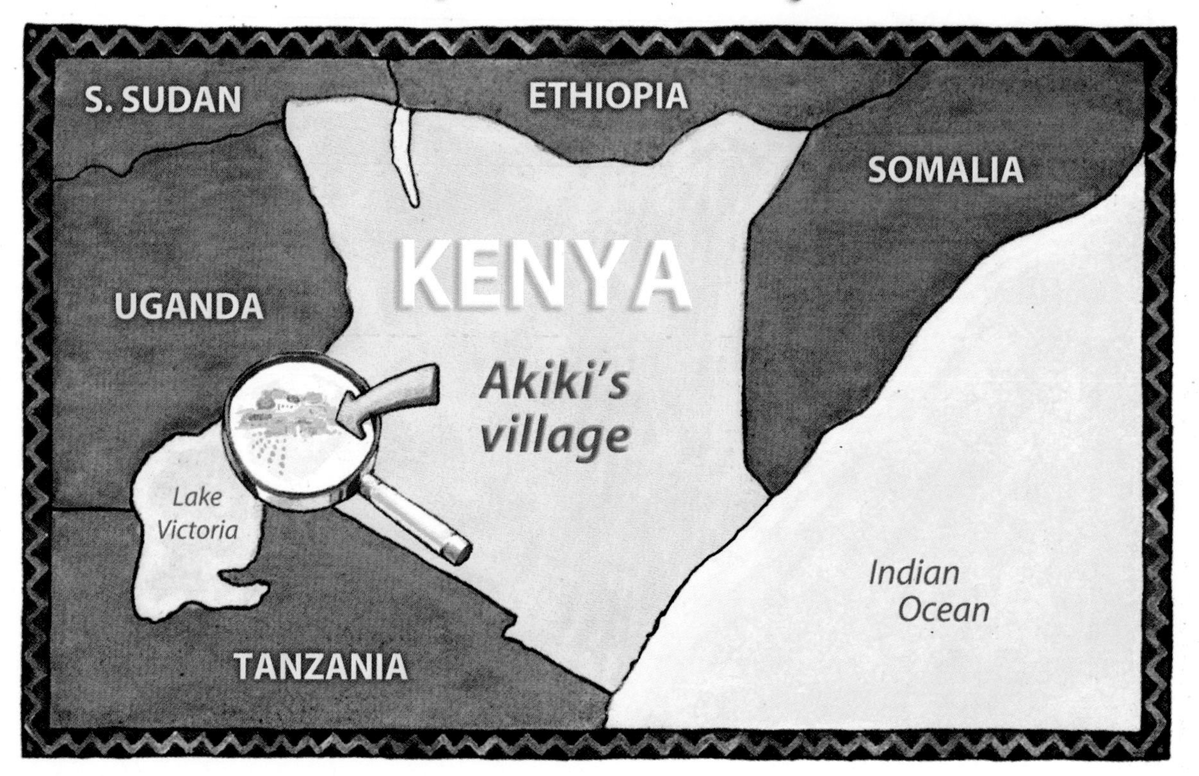

Swahili to English Dictionary

Gunia: Woven sack used for carrying grains and other dried foods

Habari: Greetings, what is new

Jembe: A garden hoe

Jiko: A small stove that uses charcoal as fuel

Mwiko: A traditional African wooden spoon used for stirring *ugali*

Posho Mill: A factory that grinds dried maize and other grains into flour

Ugali: An African firm cake-like dish made out of maize flour

Shamba: Garden, farm

Sukuma Wiki: Kale, a green leafy vegetable much like spinach

Tumbo: Stomach